My Detective Adventure

ME
AND
THE GREAT
MONSTER MYSTERY

This story
was especially written
for
Ryan Healey

D1315073

Written by Margaret Gibson
Illustrated by Ester Kasepuu & Jann McKay

It was a dark night and mysterious things were happening in a house in Orange.

'Quick, Ryan!' said a voice on the telephone. 'This is your partner, Zap. We need the help of a super detective.'

'I'll be right over,' said Ryan.
So he put on his detective disguise: a large trench coat with a high turned-up collar, gloves and dark glasses. He pulled his hat down over his forehead.

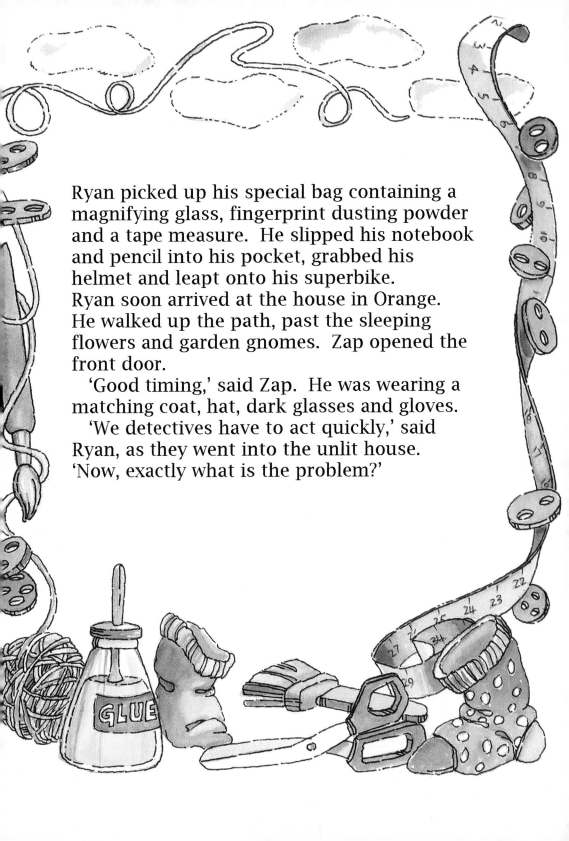

Ryan picked up his special bag containing a magnifying glass, fingerprint dusting powder and a tape measure. He slipped his notebook and pencil into his pocket, grabbed his helmet and leapt onto his superbike. Ryan soon arrived at the house in Orange. He walked up the path, past the sleeping flowers and garden gnomes. Zap opened the front door.

'Good timing,' said Zap. He was wearing a matching coat, hat, dark glasses and gloves.

'We detectives have to act quickly,' said Ryan, as they went into the unlit house. 'Now, exactly what is the problem?'

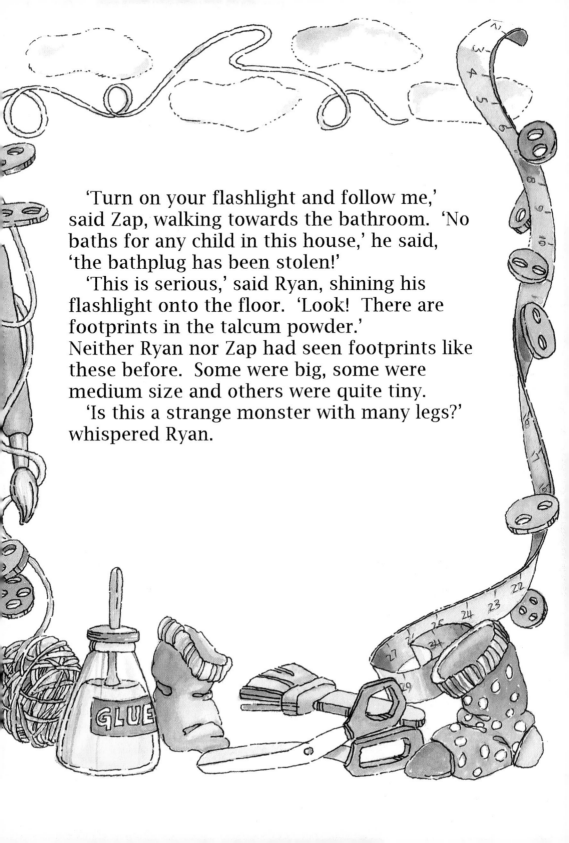

'Turn on your flashlight and follow me,' said Zap, walking towards the bathroom. 'No baths for any child in this house,' he said, 'the bathplug has been stolen!'

'This is serious,' said Ryan, shining his flashlight onto the floor. 'Look! There are footprints in the talcum powder.' Neither Ryan nor Zap had seen footprints like these before. Some were big, some were medium size and others were quite tiny.

'Is this a strange monster with many legs?' whispered Ryan.

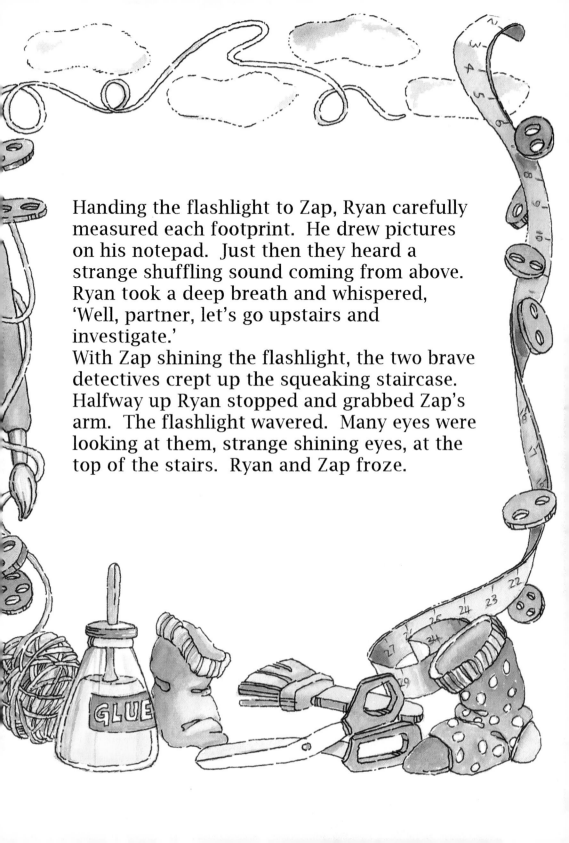

Handing the flashlight to Zap, Ryan carefully measured each footprint. He drew pictures on his notepad. Just then they heard a strange shuffling sound coming from above. Ryan took a deep breath and whispered, 'Well, partner, let's go upstairs and investigate.'

With Zap shining the flashlight, the two brave detectives crept up the squeaking staircase. Halfway up Ryan stopped and grabbed Zap's arm. The flashlight wavered. Many eyes were looking at them, strange shining eyes, at the top of the stairs. Ryan and Zap froze.

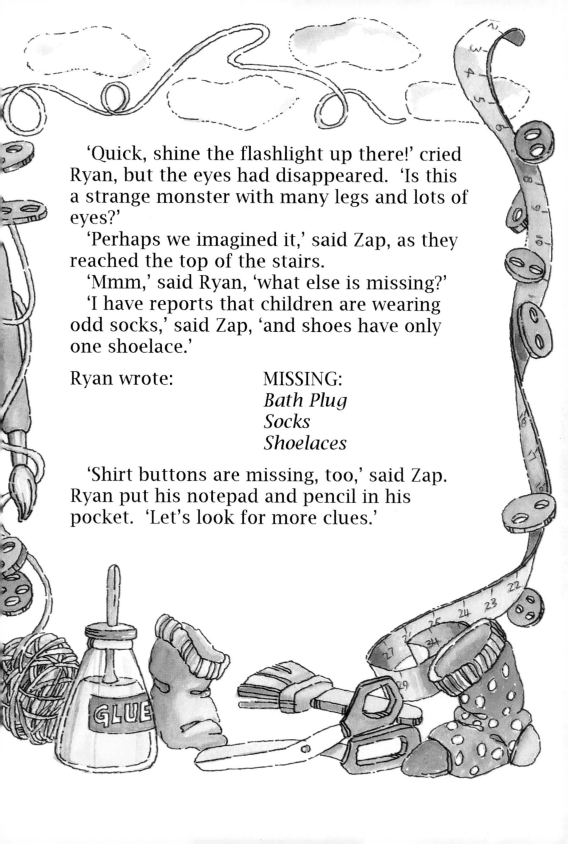

'Quick, shine the flashlight up there!' cried Ryan, but the eyes had disappeared. 'Is this a strange monster with many legs and lots of eyes?'

'Perhaps we imagined it,' said Zap, as they reached the top of the stairs.

'Mmm,' said Ryan, 'what else is missing?'

'I have reports that children are wearing odd socks,' said Zap, 'and shoes have only one shoelace.'

Ryan wrote:

MISSING:
Bath Plug
Socks
Shoelaces

'Shirt buttons are missing, too,' said Zap. Ryan put his notepad and pencil in his pocket. 'Let's look for more clues.'

They tiptoed to a door and gently pushed it open. The beam of their flashlight picked out a jumble of toys and clothes.

'Just look at the mess!' said Ryan. 'My bedroom never looks like this. What *has* been happening here?' He felt a hand reach into his pocket.

'Use your own notebook and pencil,' he said to Zap, rather crossly.

'What are you talking about?' said Zap. The two detectives stared at each other in the dim flashlight. Ryan felt in his pocket. His notepad and pencil had disappeared! Zap was so frightened that he dropped the flashlight. Then suddenly:

Many little hands pushed against Ryan's and Zap's knees. Then they heard the sound of many feet running down the dark stairs.

'So, it's a strange monster with many legs, many eyes and lots of hands,' said Ryan taking a deep breath, 'and it's not very tall.' Zap was amazed. 'That sounds like great detective work, partner. How have you reached this conclusion?'

'The hands only reached our knees,' said Ryan, 'so it has to be small.'
Just then a picture of the strange monster came into Ryan's head and he didn't feel quite so brave.

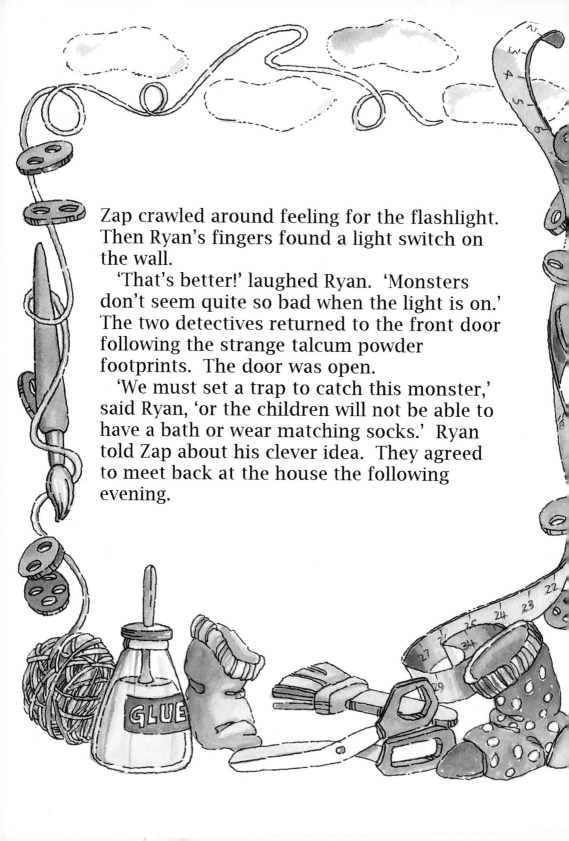

Zap crawled around feeling for the flashlight. Then Ryan's fingers found a light switch on the wall.

'That's better!' laughed Ryan. 'Monsters don't seem quite so bad when the light is on.' The two detectives returned to the front door following the strange talcum powder footprints. The door was open.

'We must set a trap to catch this monster,' said Ryan, 'or the children will not be able to have a bath or wear matching socks.' Ryan told Zap about his clever idea. They agreed to meet back at the house the following evening.

Early next morning, Ryan called all his
friends, especially Olivia, Marissa and Justin,
to his home at 78 Hampton Close, Orange. In
his best detective voice Ryan told them all
about the strange monster with many legs,
many eyes and lots of hands, and his special
plan to catch it. Everyone agreed that it was
a very clever idea. Ryan read out his long list
of the special items they would need.
The children immediately searched for lots of

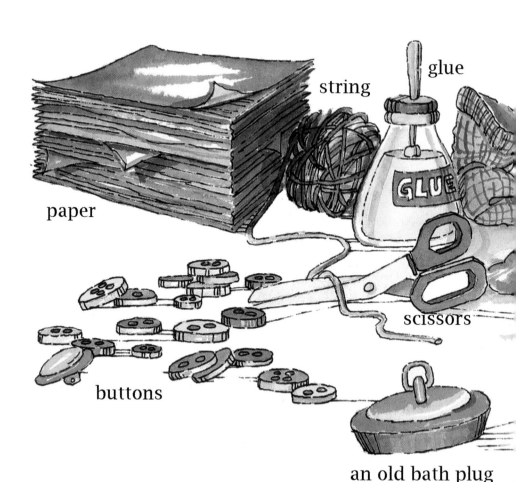

glue

string

paper

scissors

buttons

an old bath plug

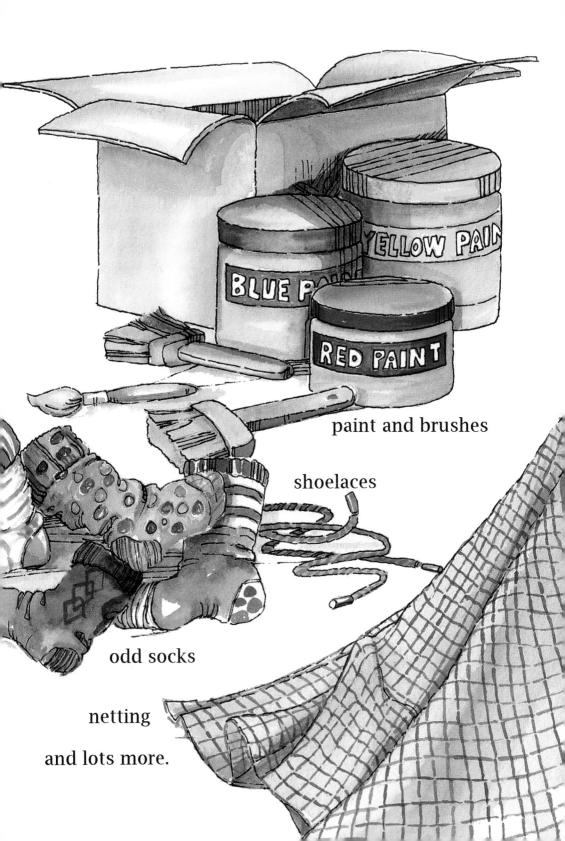

YELLOW PAINT

BLUE PAINT

RED PAINT

paint and brushes

shoelaces

odd socks

netting

and lots more.

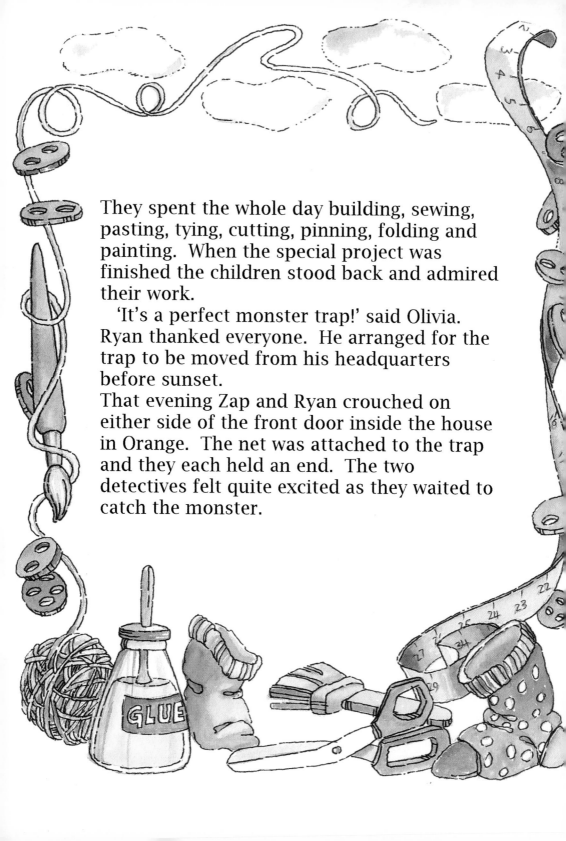

They spent the whole day building, sewing, pasting, tying, cutting, pinning, folding and painting. When the special project was finished the children stood back and admired their work.

'It's a perfect monster trap!' said Olivia. Ryan thanked everyone. He arranged for the trap to be moved from his headquarters before sunset.

That evening Zap and Ryan crouched on either side of the front door inside the house in Orange. The net was attached to the trap and they each held an end. The two detectives felt quite excited as they waited to catch the monster.

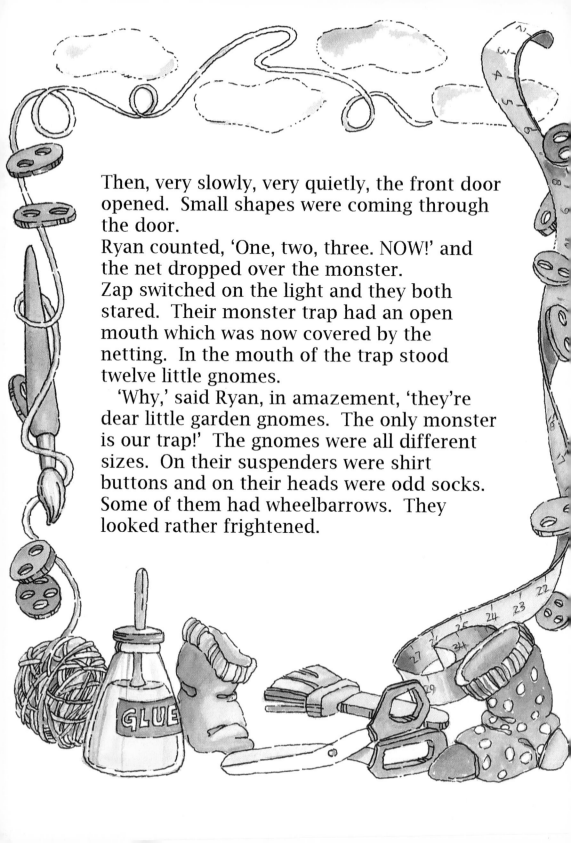

Then, very slowly, very quietly, the front door opened. Small shapes were coming through the door.

Ryan counted, 'One, two, three. NOW!' and the net dropped over the monster.

Zap switched on the light and they both stared. Their monster trap had an open mouth which was now covered by the netting. In the mouth of the trap stood twelve little gnomes.

'Why,' said Ryan, in amazement, 'they're dear little garden gnomes. The only monster is our trap!' The gnomes were all different sizes. On their suspenders were shirt buttons and on their heads were odd socks. Some of them had wheelbarrows. They looked rather frightened.

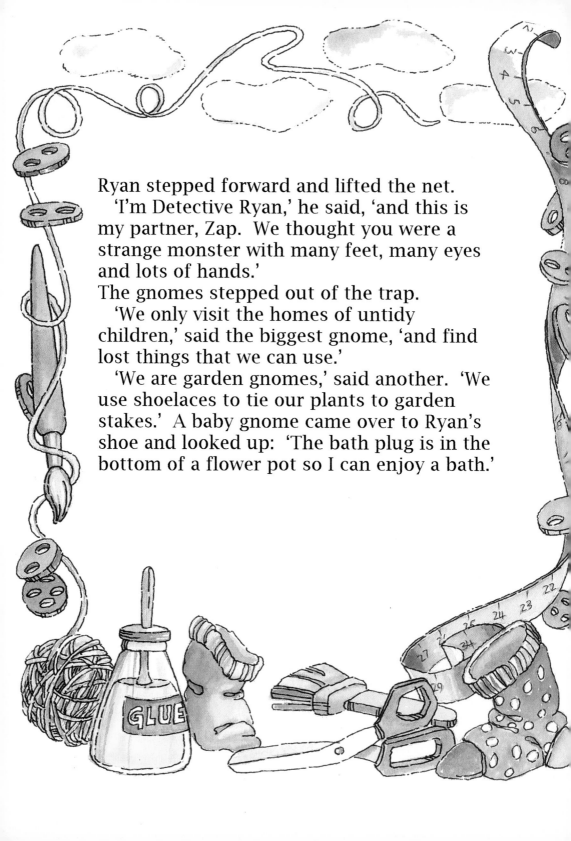

Ryan stepped forward and lifted the net.

'I'm Detective Ryan,' he said, 'and this is my partner, Zap. We thought you were a strange monster with many feet, many eyes and lots of hands.'

The gnomes stepped out of the trap.

'We only visit the homes of untidy children,' said the biggest gnome, 'and find lost things that we can use.'

'We are garden gnomes,' said another. 'We use shoelaces to tie our plants to garden stakes.' A baby gnome came over to Ryan's shoe and looked up: 'The bath plug is in the bottom of a flower pot so I can enjoy a bath.'

Just then Ryan noticed a little gnome brushing away tears.

'Whatever is the matter?' asked Ryan.

'I've broken garden gnome rules,' sobbed the little gnome, as he handed back Ryan's notebook and pencil. 'We must never steal, we can only borrow lost things from messy houses.'

'Thank you,' smiled Ryan. 'The children who live here will be much tidier from now on,' he said. 'You will have to find another untidy house.' The gnomes looked at the monster trap and started talking among themselves.

'You can pull apart my real monster now and use all the bits and pieces,' said Ryan. 'The monster mystery is solved.'

The garden gnomes laughed and started pulling off all the buttons, stacking them into their wheelbarrows. Zap and Ryan said goodbye to the little gnomes.

The great detectives felt rather tired. They wanted to get some sleep before it was time for breakfast. Ryan waved goodbye to Zap as he rode home to his headquarters. He felt very happy. Another case closed. Another job well done!